I0625864

SCI-FI SERIES 2

"I have always loved reading Stan I.S. Law's works. These stories are wonderfully crafted, chock full of visions of how Law sees the future, the fantastical science-fiction that becomes reality for the characters. Law does a wonderful job of bringing the reader into the worlds he has created, making it easy to envision yourself in each of these three environments. A highly enjoyable read!"

Catherine M. Edwards, author

"I always enjoy Law's books. They are full of esoteric thoughts, interesting and scientifically sound concepts and intriguing characters. There is religion, spirituality, science, family, friendship, heartache, passion, attraction, compassion, exploration and so much more.

This is another great contribution by Stan I.S. Law. As always I am impressed with Law's work and look forward to more. I highly recommend it!"

Ally McMahon, author

Sci-Fi Series 2

Anthology of Short Stories

Stan I.S. Law

Published by

INHOUSEPRESS

ISBN 978-1-987864-23-6

CONTENTS

***

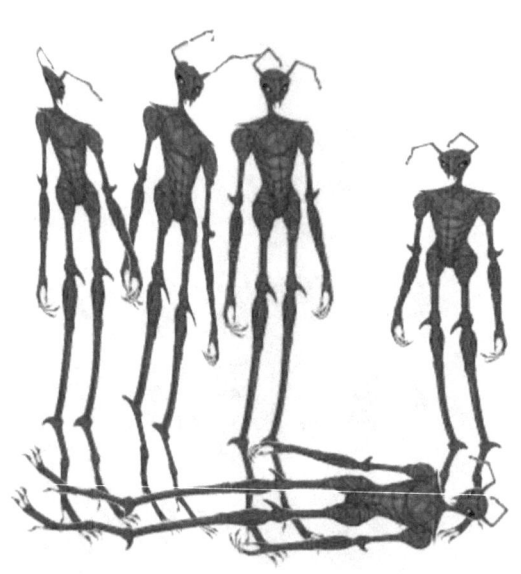

Simulator

There was nothing human about the scream.

In near total darkness, where even the stars had forsaken their shimmering sheen, within the hot breath of the steaming, churning volcanic hot springs, Astrid could only imagine the alien features contracted in a spasm of agony. Pain is pain by any other name. It hurts as much, no matter what the species. A shriek, a short silence, then a protracted whimper.

"It makes your blood curl," Astrid threw over her shoulder, busy adjusting the sensors for a directional response. "Thou shalt not interfere", she thought momentarily. The Simulator. The same instant she dismissed the conditioned response as inapplicable.

"Did you get the location?" Bram asked, his voice sleepy and definitely tired. Normally, they both slept during the night, like any normal human being should. The sensors would record any unusual sounds for later analyses. After all, they were only conducting the first, cursory scan—a very preliminary survey. Later, teams of scientists, not to mention the robo-satellites, would do their job, methodically, if necessary, over a number of years.

The Navy was hungry for new planets suitable for colonization. Hungry—but not desperate. Also, at Headquarters, they were always thinking ahead. Man finally achieved the dubious distinction of beating rabbits at their game. In spite of the sad Earth experience... The last robosat Census accounted for 57 billion souls on seventeen planets. Three point five billion per G type planet was regarded as optimum for maintaining an ecological balance. Anything over that, and... The safety margin was running out.

"Got it," she replied proudly.

After all, this was her very first mission. Acting ensign Astrid Dwain finally got her wings. Figuratively speaking, of course. But floating in a silent, near-invisible skimmer over an alien planet was the next best thing to really flying. Like in Outer Space. All the same, she loved it. Still does.

"Shouldn't we leave it till tomorrow?"

Lieutenant Jordan really needed some sleep. The last six days were tough. Six days *and* nights. Even then, it simply wasn't enough time to gather enough data to decide on the allocation of millions of credits to be expended on further study.

"I dare say, sir. But if you don't mind, I would like to get..." Astrid was exited. This was the last day of the prelimscan. It was also the first time she managed to get hold of the controls. And that only because Bram was too sleepy and tired to do the job himself.

"Whatever you'd like to get, get it quietly," Bram interrupted, and turned his back on the cabin. His bunk was on the port side. Astrid's on the starboard. The middle was no man's land. Astrid sighed haltingly. She wished it hadn't been. At nineteen, being alone with a lieutenant in a small cabin, for a whole week, meant intimacy. At least to her, it did.

All the same, she was not going to let go of her chance so easily. This guttural shriek deserved a further study. Right now. She adjusted the skimmer to drift slowly towards the source of the distraught noise. Apart from her own pleasure, there was an added advantage to night study. In daytime, they could only scan the terrain from an altitude of a few kilometers. At night, with the cooler temperature creating a protective mist, the skimmer could descent practically to the treetops. Even lower. Not only the minutest details would show up on the screens, but they could also record the sounds. They had to be careful, of course. Very careful.

She was well aware of the eleventh commandment among men of Old Earth, the first among the anthropologists: "Thou shalt not interfere". For a thousand and one reasons—there could be no extenuating circumstances for breaking this archaic law. In early twenty-second century, three planets had plunged into a genocidal warfare, all thanks to the help received from the concerned, 'advanced' civilization. From the Almighty Man. Later on, that same century, a planet, in the 3rd quadrant of the 24th sector, boiled. Literally boiled, when an aspiring student had magnanimously donated water, in the form of rain, to a large group of indigenous, primitive yet undoubtedly sentient beings, apparently on the verge of dying of thirst. The student had done so before the full geological survey had come in. Later, they had learned that there had been lime, quicklime, masked over large areas by no more than a foot thick layer of soil. And lime mixed with water, had a predictable, if unpleasant effect. It never rained on that planet.

Catastrophes of this magnitude could now be averted. The generosity of the students of anthropology, on occasion, could not. Ever since people on Old Earth got fed up with being restricted to protective shells of domes, which filtered the relentless cosmic bombardment. It could be said that the loss of the ozone layer was the single most powerful stimulus for man venturing to the stars. From that moment on, a 'moment' spanning some four decades, man developed an insatiable appetite for other type G planets, suitable for colonization. Hence the students. They performed a very necessary, even if, on occasion, slightly overanxious function. Students loved to experiment. Their parents preferred making money.

The latest discs on anthropology had given Astrid strong indications that no mater what the species, the basic steps of evolution invariably followed a similar pattern; regardless of the initial, or for that matter ultimate, shape, type, protective wrapping, bone structure, or the number of arms or legs. Once the genetic chain, the incisive genome, had been activated, the evolution could not be halted. The physiological form of the species had often been the result of geophysical accidents rather than of any particular biological preference. The only criteria which nature appeared to consider valid in advancing the evolution of any one species over another, were traits of adaptability that assured survival. Darwin had once called it the Survival of the Fittest. It still held true. On all the planets. Time took care of the rest. Time and challenges.

"You're not going to follow up on that scream,

are you?" Bram interrupted her thoughts, again, his voice sounding as hopeful as it was fatigued.

"I'll call you if I need you, sir. I'll be as quiet as a mouse," she replied. Were mice that quiet? You should hear mice on Gemini Four. You could hear them for half a mile!

Lieutenant Bram Jordan was her senior. In fact he was not only a lieutenant in the Galactic Navy but he also held a B.Sc. in anthropology. She, Astrid Dwain, was an ensign. An acting ensign and a student. "And if its the last thing I do," she muttered to herself, "I'll make him notice me, *and* my work, before this night is out. Dam it, I am nineteen, and I could hardly shake off all the cadets at the Academy, this last year. And this, this... well, he doesn't even know that I am a woman."

Astrid bit her full lips in stubborn determination and returned to her work. Within seconds she heard the slow, regular breathing of her, let's face it, undeniably attractive if inconsiderate companion. Soon, however, her youthful resilience took over as her mind continued to spin an endemic web of evolution.

In all her previous experience, albeit academic, it had been the challenges, the adversities, which were the single, most prominent factor in the rate of advancement of any particular species. Of the races she'd studied, including Homo sapiens, she detected little, if any, evolutionary progress during times of geological, climatic or social calm. On the other hand, any upheavals, any major difficulties, later even wars, which tested to the utmost the resources of the incipient mind of a primitive, awakening intelligence, resulted in evolutionary leaps of truly inspiring magnitude. This was even true of Man reaching for the stars. He hadn't until he had to.

Hence, the Law of Noninterference. Do not help until asked, and even then be prepared for taking responsibility for your actions. To assure a strict conformance with this Law, the Headquarters had developed a method, whereby they could, and did, subject an errant student of anthropology to the medicine to which he or she had subjected others through his or her indiscretion.

Astrid had known all that when she'd accepted, joyously, her appointment to assist in the preliminary anthropological review of the fourth planet of the DM45 star, in the 27th sector. The planet of the Gharrs. The sound represented by these letters: 'GHARR', was the only sound they had managed to record on the audio-scanners. A deep, throaty, guttural sound. Hence Gharrs. What else could one call them?

After full six days of round the clock scanning,

the planet had shown hardly any signs of even embryonic intelligence. Certainly not in the behavioral pattern of the natives. The skimmer had recorded, however, some configurations of terrain that indicated an awareness of rudimentary geometrical forms. No construction, per se, just forms. For the moment, they could not dismiss the evidence. Pity, since type G planets were relatively scarce. Type G's could support human life without any major terra-forming adaptations. The gravity had to be within plus or minus ten percent of the earth. The air had to be breathable, the water potable. The temperature range had been regarded as secondary. Within reason, of course. The rest would take care of itself. Assuming no deadly bacteria, plague causing viruses and such like, such planets represented ready-made gardens of Eden. There remained only the question of any intelligent life indigenous to the planet. That possibility was the sole reason for the vigilant eye being maintained for extended periods over a prospective site for colonization. Man was ever ready to extend his hungry tentacles, to expand his galactic domain. But the Law of Noninterference could not be ignored nor bypassed. In the long run, diversity of life forms was considered the best assurance of man's survival, even if only the solons understood the logic of this statement.

Again her scanners picked up a long, sustained whimper. Following the first scream of agony, once she was sure that Bram was asleep, Astrid had turned up the volume, slightly, on the audio-scanners. She tuned them to record only the sound waves originating from Gharrs. It was not a full-proof method, but it helped to eliminate up to ninety percent of extraneous noises. So far, the most peculiar characteristic of the planet was that, above the level of tiny insects, the Gharrs were the only living species living on this ball of dust. This fact alone made the planet, and the Gharrs, unique.

Astrid calculated that the origin of the distressed cry was no more than four kilometers west/north/west from their present location. She set the skimmer to home in on the source of the last guttural sound emission. Skimmers were very fast along the up and down axis. The nullgravs made sure of that. In the horizontal direction, however, they were really floaters. Silent, near-invisible, and very slow.

No matter how primitive a society, there those rare, Special Occasions, when group psychosis, or perhaps a certain, inexplicable *gestält* can be felt, even by outsiders. As Astrid drifted towards her coordinates, this undefined sensation grew stronger.

While the swirling fog offered her craft virtually

total protection from being seen by the natives, her infrared viewers afforded her perfect opportunity to study the terrain. In no time at all, the automatic scanners detected a number of natives converging towards a single point, or at least to a single, well defined area. Within ten more minutes it became evident that the point of convergence was a raised plateau, which Bram had recorded earlier this week. The center of the mount was, in itself, a source of considerable heat emission. The raised ground was a large, almost perfect circle, about a hundred meters in diameter. In the center of the podium the ground rose another three meters in two stages, creating a stepped, if rather flat, pyramid. It seemed destined to serve some kind of a ceremonial purpose. Judging by a thick layer of cinders, whatever the ritual, it had something to do with fire.

Astrid had to keep the skimmer at a discrete distance from the fire itself. The Law of Noninterference was quite explicit about not being seen. The last anthropological team who had been spotted by the natives at a distant planet, became immortalized by them as gods, thus enriching the indigent lore, but delaying the primitive culture's progress by quite a few centuries. Astrid had no intention of committing such an error. Not during her very first time at the controls. What was more, she felt it in her bones that if she played her cards right, this night's recording would leave Bram in awe of her work. He would notice her, dammit! He bloody well would.

For a moment her thoughts drifted to the main hall, at the Academy. She saw herself, standing to attention, facing rows upon rows of cadets, all admiring, spellbound, while she is decorated for the exemplary excellence of her work, her devotion to duty, her... Then the Admiral Artemis, himself, announces her promotion to Ensign First Class, perhaps a Second Lieutenant, perhaps... She would become an officer. Bram would have to return her salute. She smiled at the thought. She made a mental note to salute him every five minutes.

By the time Astrid settled her skimmer into a hovering mode, a group of some fifty natives already began their throaty, halting chanting. There was no beauty to their song that she could perceive. If anything, she sensed something halfway between anger and supplication. The natives, ever reinforced by new arrivals, now began a slow, rhythmic dance, consisting mainly of stumping their feet, clapping their hands together in front of them, while passing over their scaly heads bits of wood toward the central fire, with their uppermost, spindly appendages. The motion was accompanied by a smooth wave of their semi-stooped bodies, bent at the hips, which had an almost hypnotic quality. Their bodies moved in perfect unison, as though an invisible conductor led this dark, nocturnal orchestra. Although Astrid had absolutely no idea what the creatures were performing on this damp, vaporous night, she felt strangely drawn into their rhythmic oscillations. She felt her body moving in accord with the wavy motion of the growing crowd.

Very slowly, very gradually, Astrid's subjective time seemed to come to a stop. Her motions became lethargic, her eyes fixed on the screen, which drew the strange ceremony into her fascinated awareness. The guttural chanting first recorded, then amplified by the speakers, filled the pure, filtered air within the skimmer with the natives' presence. After a short, undefined while, Astrid felt that she could smell, almost inhale, the thick, sweet, steamy air outside the confines of her micro-environment. The flickering light of the flames, picked up by the infrared scanners, projected from the screens and danced on the walls of the small cabin. Astrid, in all but physical body, took part in the esoteric, incomprehensible ceremony.

"So what happened to him?"

The voice came from the darkness behind her.

She almost panicked before realizing that Bram had woken up. No wonder, the speakers were now almost on full volume. Had she turned them on so loud?

"What happened to the poor blighter?" he repeated.

Astrid turned down the speakers. She felt a powerful, evocative need to converge on the top of the mound. The top of the pyramid. All should converge there. All who were within the sound of the chanting.

"Ah, who, what blighter...?"

Her mind refused to give up its mesmeric attraction. She was still, more than just partially, absorbed in the intensity of concentration, focusing all her thoughts at the very centre of the Fire. It was the one Power which could, and did, pierce the convoluting vapors. Yes, that's what it was. The Altar of Fire. It cleansed all that came in contact with it. Even by proxy. Even if only by a piece of wood passed overhead in a sacred, worshiping wave of absolute submission.

"The poor thing that emitted that shrill noise. Before you told me to go to sleep." Bram sat up on one elbow. "Are you all right, ensign?"

"I am perfectly all right, thank you lieutenant," Astrid answered in a stilted, over precise tone. What is the matter with him? Doesn't he know my name?

Ensign? "I thought you were going to sleep?"

"I was, until your cacophony had woken me up. Take it easy, ensign. I know that this is the last night, but only of this preliminary survey—not of the world." Bram turned back to face the wall.

That remark, that asinine, insidious remark, removed the rest of her cobwebs. Instantly.

Couldn't he at least have asked me what I had been doing? Not that I want any interruptions, but it would be polite. After all, I too had spent, these last few days, all the waking hours assisting him. And we did collect more data than could possibly have been expected after only a preliminary scantrip. I wouldn't be at all surprised if he didn't get another stripe on his sleeve for all the hours we'd both put in. I wouldn't be at all surprised.

At the time, Astrid did not appreciate how lucky she was that Bram's questions had pulled her out of the mesmeric hold of the throaty chanting below them. For a while, she wondered about her superior officer. She couldn't see his features, but they were firmly etched in her memory. A lean, almost skinny face, hunched down, for interminable hours, over the keyboard controlling the various scanners. His back bent at almost a right angle. Frankly, he was much too tall to work at standard keyboard level. The skimmers were designed for men not exceeding 1.85

meters. Bram had been born on a planet of 0.78 earth gravity. She had learned that much in the Academy. They all learned the vital statistic of all the officers in the survey teams. By the time Bram was twenty, he had shot up to over two meters in his bare feet. With new colonial regulations in place, this could not happen. Plus or minus ten percent Earth gravity, was the present norm. At least, for the last fifteen years. All the same, herself being blond, blue eyed and tiny, she was fascinated by this lanky, wiry dark man, who could walk faster then most people could run.

Then her eyes returned to the dials. She waited until Bram's breathing indicated that he was asleep again. In a way, she was grateful to him. Somehow, she did not feel like sharing with anyone this strange, compelling occasion. She refused to share it with him, yet she felt she had been sharing it with.... by now, some three to four hundred natives. Her slim fingers dialed the keyboard for the census scanner. Four hundred and forty seven life forms. And they were still coming. Droves of them. Perhaps she ought to wake the lieutenant. This gathering was quite unprecedented.

No, I bloody well will not, she rebelled. After all, in his mind, I probably don't really exist!

I wonder what is the peculiar force of the Gharrs' chanting...

She could only guess at the answer to this enigma. There had been no precedent.

Then Astrid remembered of what Bram had reminded her about. Almost against her will, she programmed the skimmer to float towards the spot where she had originally recorded the native emitting the guttural shriek and whimper. The craft floated silently to hover over the coordinates. She examined the ground directly beneath her. It had not been difficult to find the poor, hapless creature.

The infrared scanners displayed on her screen an alien, its hind legs caught in a tapering crevice, between two rocks. In its attempts to free itself, it must have wedged itself even deeper between the harsh, volcanic stone surfaces. The bioscanners indicated a lowered temperature of the creature. Lower than that of the other aliens. The poor blighter, as Bram had called him, must have fainted, or was on the verge of dying. If it was already dead, she could extract its body with the tractor beam. But if it was dead, what would be the point? There was a point. They could dissect it and learn, perhaps a lot, from it.

And if it was not dead, what would the Law have to say about it? The Law of Noninterference applied only to intelligent species. The throaty chanting did not offer any conclusive evidence about the sentience of the creatures. Many animals on Earth, used to produce quite a variety of sounds in their attempts at communication. That alone did not define intelligence. In fact, a precise definition has eluded the scientists for centuries. With intelligent life throughout the galaxy manifesting itself in so many different forms, no one wanted to limit, let alone define, the term 'intelligence'. Except for the psychoscans.

But here, the Gharrs had not raised any buildings, there were no roads or identifiable tracks of overland communications, no towns or villages or any visible signs of any centers of communal living. Just the raised, flat pyramids, which would go practically unnoticed if it hadn't been for today's fire. Even fire itself was no indication of their sentience, since the number of active and semi-active volcanoes could easily have provided the source of fire even as the rivers offered the source of water. What then of the hypnotic chanting?

Astrid decided to grab her opportunity when it presented itself. To study the body of an indigent life form so soon after its death could yield some valid information. By now its body temperature has dropped by eleven degrees. It must have died even as, on other scanners, she watched the distant, ever growing fire. She began to feel guilty. If it had not been a sentient life form, she could have helped it.

And if it had been? What of it? What of the
Simulator? She would be forced to experience the act
of being helped by someone. That could not possibly
be that unpleasant. Now the creature was dead.
Regardless of its intelligence, or lack of it. Thanks to
her. Thanks to her weakness of allowing her to be
distracted, and attracted, to the inimitable chanting.

Astrid decided to seize the body of the dark
scaled, four armed and two-legged creature for later
study. She programmed the tractor beams, lifted the
body as gently as possible, so as not to injure it in the
process of extricating it from the crevice. She
secreted and secured the carcass in the main holding
area below the floor of the skimmer. Wiping
perspiration from her brow, she floated slowly
towards the chanting crowd.

The tribe, the herd, the mob, whatever they
would turn out to be, appeared to have stabilized at
about six hundred. The olfactory sensors detected a
new scent in the steamy, moldy air. Astrid dialed for
a sample. She sniffed it gingerly and fought back
nausea. It smelled like burned flesh. My God, she
thought, some poor blighter must have fallen into the
fire! Not a very good sign of rudimentary
intelligence. The smell persisted. Intensified. More
bodies? Cleansing by Fire? Rites of purification?
Primitive, barbaric, but not unheard of. What were

these creatures doing? Before Astrid left to pick up the body of the unlucky screamer, she remembered an elusive feeling that the celebrations were, in some way, connected with an act or function of expurgation. But what animals purify themselves by throaty singing? Sentient or not, the creatures presented an enigma.

She glanced at her watch. There was less then an hour left before daylight. It was time to leave the natives to their chanting and drift upwards to a safer altitude. She also needed rest. Since Bram and she were dropped on the planet six days ago, she didn't have a chance to do much sleeping. She tried as hard anyone can to create an impression. Quite true, on Bram Jordan. And why not? He was young, a full lieutenant, already had an academic reputation, and, well, she just loved those long, powerful legs of his. He was known in the whole of the Academy as the best climber in all the seventeen Systems. They said that he took up mountaineering to build up muscles after having been born on a low gravity planet. He sure as hell built them up. And down. Lets face it, the man was darn attractive. And this was their last day together. Unless...

For all she knew, the Headquarters might well decide to wait a few hundred years before the first attempt at colonization. They had to be sure about the natives, and, there was a slight latent radiation in a number of depressed areas of the planet. Particularly areas adjacent to large estuaries. Who knows? It might wear off—in time. Or it could be indigenous to the planet.

The skimmer began rising. She could climb very fast, but the inertia would wake up Bram. She didn't feel like being lectured again. The skimmer rose gently, like a hawk soaring on a rising air current, a chimney under some cirrus cotton wool creampuffs. She stretched herself on the bunk opposite Bram's. There was little she could do now but wait. Tomorrow they would photograph the site of the nocturnal fire. During daytime, with the fog lifting, the film would provide all the data she may have missed. She relaxed with a satisfying feeling of a work well done. Finally, she could give her sore eyes a well-deserved rest. They itched from watching the screen displays as well as from sheer lack of sleep. She stretched out in the Spartan luxury of her resilient bunk.

She slept within seconds.

It seemed, that almost at once, a rhythmic, staccato chanting invaded her inner, chimerical universe. She tossed and turned, getting little rest, in spite of her fatigue. Then, she heard the original shriek of pain. It filled her, saturated her, as though she was in its very centre. As if it was she who had been screaming. She sat up on her bunk, her forehead moist, her teeth clenched. She glanced at the altimeter. Five thousand forty meters, and rising. And then, she heard the agonizing, drawn out, guttural scream again. This time she was wide, very wide-awake.

It was the same excruciating scream, which had initiated her research, although on this occasion, she sensed more horror or panic in it than pain. For a brief moment, she hoped that she had been still dreaming. A sad, lonesome whine followed the plaintive, throaty cry. Then, another guttural sound resounded, practically within the cabin. By the time she stood up, Bram was sitting up on his bunk, looking baffled.

"Astrid... what in the name of heavens, it this?" He really was perplexed. The interior of the skimmer had been well insulated from such ungainly sounds.

By then, Astrid was in command of her senses. She looked at her watch. There was no time to explain. She had ten minutes to sunrise. The deep fog would begin rising in less than ten minutes.

"Put on your security straps. Now!" She almost shouted when Bram didn't move. He did not expect to take orders. His eyebrows questioning, he did as he was told.

The same instant Astrid punched the keyboard with grim determination. The skimmer was in free-fall. Directly downwards. She pulled up to a silent stop two feet above the ground. The hold trap doors opened and the alien's body was deposited on the sodden ground. A second later, the skimmer was rising at a velocity equal to the previous descent.

"For crying out loud, can't you take it a bit easy?" Bram looked a little sick. "This is a skimmer, not a bloody rocket!"

The whole maneuver took less then two minutes. To use a tractor beam to deposit the native on the ground would not have taken any longer. But tractor beam is visible at night, and Astrid wanted to deposit the creature as close as possible to the still chanting crowd. That way, if her temporary guest had been maimed, or otherwise injured, it could be helped by its comrades. If they did help each other. It had not been a very profound and thought out decision, but Astrid felt a little guilty for having been sidetracked by the fire dance from her original purpose, which had been to see what happened to a screaming native. She felt that by her actions she had made up, at least in part, for her earlier indiscretion. In the meantime, she set the scanners to continue recording the activities of the celebration. She needed sleep. Badly.

"What happened?" Bram was still sitting, strapped, on his bunk.

First time in a week, Astrid had actually forgotten about Bram Jordan. "Oh, I am sorry, sir. Do take off those straps. You look ridiculous in them." She giggled. Her nerves were exhausted. The rest of her body followed close behind. She left the controls and staggered to her bunk. She practically collapsed on it. With a last ditch effort, she turned to her superior.

"It's all on the discs, sir." She looked like a little girl, her blue irises hardly visible through the small slits of her swollen eyes. "I'll be back soon, sir." With that her eyes closed and stayed closed for the next four hours. By the time she was ready to open them again, the orbiting spaceship's tractor beam was ready to pick them up. Her first mission had been over.

One month later, the Navy Headquarters had decided to leave the fourth planet in the DM45 solar system, the planet of the Gharrs alone—for a while. Admittedly, it was a type G planet, but there was the question of the latent radiation. Not enough to be dangerous but also not conducive to a feeling of absolute safety. The robo-satellites would maintain a steady watch on the new discovery. Who knows, the radiation could dissipate in a decade or two. Or in a hundred years. For a while the Headquarters could not decide what to make of it. Not until they examined the psychoscan.

The disciplinary hearing was fairly brief. The Dean of anthropology, two captains of the Galactic Navy Survey Corps and the Acting Admiral in charge. The table, semicircular, gave all the members of the Quorum a perfect view of, and a direct relationship to, the two members of the survey team under investigation.

"The accused shall rise." Admiral Alton Archemis ordered. He pressed the button of the recording machine. The hearing was in session.

Lieutenant Bram Jordan and Acting Ensign Astrid Dwain stood to attention.

"You are hereby charged with having breached paragraph seventeen, subparagraph twelve of the Naval Code, referred to as the Law of Noninterference. You have been served with the writ twenty-one days ago. Did you have time to review the charge?" The question was rhetorical. All writs are served with a twenty-one days notice. The Admiral played by the book.

Bram, still standing to attention, addressed the Quorum.

"Permission to address the Court?" Although he

really addressed the Admiral, Bram followed the established procedure

Admiral Archemis glanced at his colleagues.

"Carry on, Lieutenant. Keep it brief." He admonished.

"Thank you sir. I shall. I wish to report, sir, I further wish to make it abundantly clear that, at the time of the infringement, I have been in sole command of the skimmer. Under the circumstances, I assume full responsibility for the said infringement and request that all charges against Acting Ensign Astrid Dwain be dropped. That is all sir!" Bram relaxed his taught body slightly. This was the second time he had to face the disciplinary committee. The first time happened when he himself had been an ensign. He was not likely to forget that experience.

"Permission to speak, Sir, ah, the Court?" Astrid stretched her body to the utmost. The top of her head barely reached to the middle chest button on Bram's full dress tunic.

The Admiral appeared to have problems keeping his face straight. The two in front of him made a most improbable couple he had ever seen. The Lieutenant looked as though he could pick the girl up with one hand, put her over his shoulder and then sprint to a new record in the hundred meters at the Galactic Games. She, on the other hand, seemed to suggest, that she might well ride the lieutenant's shoulders, rather like a proficient equestrian rides a noble if unwilling stallion.

"Yes, Ensign Dwain, what is it?" His voice was almost paternal.

"I wish to report, sir, that at the time of the said infringement, Lieutenant Bram Jordan had been sound asleep. I respectfully submit, sir, that under no circumstances can he be held accountable for the infringement, which I have committed completely under my own, I mean, on my own, sir!" Her cheeks were as red as her pouting mouth.

"Is that all, chil... Ensign Dwain?" Admiral Archemis had a daughter about Astrid's age. She had broken many 'infringements' at home. He often wished, his rank counted for something during the after duty hours.

"Yes sir!" Ensign Dwain had finished.

"Very well. You will both retire to the adjacent booths and put on the helmets. We shall render our decision."

The dreaded helmets did not have to be dreaded. There was a vast application for them in the course of training at the Academy. The large, conical contraptions stimulated the neurons to absorb direct experience programming. They insinuated events directly to the brain cells. Whatever had been taught this way gave the recipient a full recollection of the events, by galvanizing all the sensory centers. The man or woman under the helmet could see, hear, feel, smell and taste the experience. Hence, the Simulator. It could be very nice. It didn't have to be.

The two culprits did not have to wait long for the Court's decision. Almost immediately Bram and Astrid felt a great sense of relaxation, and then their awareness shifted to a different world at a different time. Their brains were hooked up directly to the psychoscan waves recorded over the Gharrs' planet. For a moment they felt lost, bewildered, and then they shared the thoughts, the feelings, the sensory inputs of the one Gharr, which they, or rather Astrid, picked up from the crevice. The images were vivid, very alien, they were looking through aboriginal, extrinsic eyes. But the essence of the communication was undeniable. Which part was true, which was the creature's imagination that could not be distinguished. If the creature had been sentient, then Bram and Astrid would be able to feel whatever the creature felt. They would share the Gharr's experience.

There were flashes, disjointed images, extracted from archaic past. There were more immediate illusions. There was the present.

"Many thousands of cycles past... a great Fire burning, scorching, destroying... all...all...all...

Purifying, poisoning... land. Purifying, poisoning water... Purifying, poisoning air, air...all air... Great, great, purifying Fire...

"Great, great, grand Fathers...Cycles, cycles... Gharr shall worship Fire... Fire shall never poison again... Never again... never... Purify, always purify...Stay close to the land...close to water. Gharr shall never rise above the moisture. Moisture surrounds all Fire... Gharr will stay low... low will last for ever, ever, ever...

"Gharr multiplies and grow and swells... Gharr survive Great Purification."

The images of the fire were frightening. Both, Bram and Astrid, cringed when they saw the very air burning. The fire was everywhere. There was nothing but fire. Burning, consuming, annihilating. Archaic, demonic memories of Dante's hell drawn from the depth of the creatures subconscious. Then, the next instant, the infernal images changed.

"I rise, I conquer, I climb, I must... Above the water...Ghaaarrrr...."

The scream of agony. Vivid, painful. Bram and Astrid felt their legs caught in a relentless vice. They each fought to free themselves, but to no avail. Their strength ebbed, drained their consciousness...

"Darkness... come... free... peace..."

Bram's helmet stopped sending messages. He

blinked hard. He was back in the here and now. His head ached. He raised the contraption and stepped out from the booth. His legs felt weak. He staggered to his chair. The Quorum had been sitting at their appointed places. Nobody smiled. Bram glanced at his watch. Three and a half minutes had passed since he entered the booth. Thought waves travel at the speed of light. Then he stiffened. Where the devil is Astrid? He looked behind him. She had just opened her booth. She staggered, almost fell. In a single leap he was at her side. He picked her up and gently deposited her in her chair, still facing their judges and their jury. Her eyes were filled with horror. But more than that, there was tremendous pain deeply etched within them. He never looked into her eyes before. My God, how blue, how very blue... What the devil had they done to her?

Admiral Artemis waited until Astrid recovered her wits, her full awareness. Then he smiled encouragement.

"That is the Simulator. As you both know, there is a good reason for it." Then he rose from behind the semicircular table and approached the two youngsters. Immediately, Bram and Astrid rose to attention. She stood very close to Bram. She didn't want to be alone on the Gharr planet again. Ever. The Admiral first faced Lieutenant Jordan.

"Commander Jordan. I wish to express our thanks for the excellent work you are doing for the Navy. You are awarded our highest recognition for your continued efforts in furthering our work of providing Mankind with room for expansion." The Admiral shook Bram's hand. There was firmness and warmth in his handshake. It was sincere. Bram had to bend down a little to allow the Admiral to append the medal.

He then turned to Astrid. She seems to have recovered, if only temporarily. The Simulator memories would linger on for a long time yet.

"Acting Ensign Dwain. I am sure you will have learned a great deal from your first experience. We cannot always do what we would like to. We are not gods. We do not command the lives of others. Nevertheless, swiftness of your reflexes, your willingness to make decisions had been noted. You are hereby promoted to Ensign, First Class, of the Galactic Navy. Congratulations." The Admiral shook Astrid's hand, looking, all along, as if he would rather kiss her on both cheeks and then sit her on his lap. Instead, the grey haired, kindly looking Admiral returned to his central chair at the table.

"By now, you must have both realized, that if it hadn't been for your, ah, infringement, we might have gone on for years, without realizing that Gharrs had developed a rudimentary sentience. Now, we know a few things about them, which I find rather fascinating. Professor Taw Ming tells us, that the Gharr specie is a very close relative to the Earth's cockroach. The fact that it had grown to be over eight feet in height, is probably the result of nuclear radiation. This thesis is supported by the fact that there are still areas where radiation lingers, particularly at such points as estuaries, the most likely site for some previous civilization which, alas, appears to have destroyed itself. I must remind you, that we, Mankind, had once been at those very crossroads. We resolved our differences, the Gharrs predecessors...

"This thesis is further reinforced by the psychogenetic memories, still powerful in the present day Gharrs. Yes, although we, to my knowledge, had not, ah.. recently, committed any infringements," he gestured at the members of the Court, "we all had donned the helmets. We consider the pain well worthwhile. We are all in your debt. Particularly yours, young lady." With that the Admiral rose.

The hearing was over.

Commander Bram Jordan and Ensign, First Class, Astrid Dwain, rose to attention. They waited until the last member of the jury left the chamber.

Bram suspected that he might well be absolved of a major infringement, but a promotion? Commander Bram Jordan. At twenty-seven, it must, surely, be something of a Naval record. Maybe now, Astrid will notice me, he thought. From the day he met her, he had been afraid to touch her, least he break one of her tiny bones. My God she was tiny. A pocket Venus. Only much, much more beautiful.

On the way to the door, the Simulator memory returned to Astrid with such force that she staggered. Bram caught her in his arms.

"It was horrible, you know, just horrible. The fire... " She sobbed on his chest.

Bram raised her in his arms as though she were a child.

"What was so horrible... the fire?" The images he had seen were certainly frightening but to him, the pain of having his feet caught in the vice of the volcanic rock was, by far, the most painful memory. Then he remembered that his helmet stopped emitting the thought waves a minute or so before hers.

"...they passed him overhead to purify him... he wanted to be purified.. he went too high, they threw him in the fire. The burning flesh... the smell...oh, it was ghastly!" She no longer even tried to hold back her tears.

"There.. there, it will go away. It will go away.

You just give it time...."

Bram carried her in his arms to the shuttle, which took them to the roof, then to his waiting, souped-up, skimmer. He did not seem aware of her weight at all. He dialed coordinates of a restaurant he knew, where he had celebrated his previous promotion. He felt she needed a strong drink. So did he, for that matter. He continued to stroke her hair so lightly, as though it had been spun from filaments of golden, brittle glass.

It's been a good ten minutes since Astrid recovered from the effects of the Simulator. It never crossed her mind to tell Bram that she was all right, now. She felt very snug and safe in his arms. The arms of Commander Jordan. The Simulator experience had been worth it after all. And anyway, why spoil a good thing when it's offered, free?

***

Little Angels

If you just sit down, Madam, the doctor will be with you momentarily."

The Little Angels Inc. prided itself on efficiency. By the time the smile faded from the vacuous, gum-chewing receptionist's face, a sonorous buzzer announced that the doctor was ready to receive the next patient. That's right, patient. Not customer. The distinction was very important. Little Angels Inc. had nothing to sell. They were in the business of helping people. And they did it much better, more efficiently, and with fewer expenses, than any of their competitors. Just read the advertisements. Anywhere.

"It was hardly worth sitting down, was it dear? There, let me give you a hand."

John helped his wife to get up. Towards the end of the eighth month, sometimes, it's not that easy.

The receptionist continued to wash and scrape away last week's crumbling red crust with evil smelling nail polish remover. "Go right in, dear." She said without taking her eyes from her absorbing work.

"Thank you," Mary whispered.

She was tired. It was true that they didn't have to wait, hardly at all, at the Little Angels, but it took them all of a four hours drive to get here.

The oversized brass plate on the oak paneled door spelled out: "DR. ALLAN D. ANGLES, and underneath the name: Doctor of Obstetric Cryogenics. John and Mary walked, arm in arm, into the doctor's office. It had to be done. They postponed the inevitable as long as they could.

The doctor got up to greet them. That was nice. No other doctor ever bothered to get up for either of them. Further more, no matter how long a time in advance they had ever made an appointment, not one of them had ever been on time. Until now. Today.

"It is good of you to see us on such a short notice," John said. "My name is..."

"John Algernon Bolton. How do you do, Sir? But it is with the young lady we are concern with here, aren't we?" The good doctor winked knowingly as he consulted his pad. "Mrs. Mary Martha Bolton. Am I right?"

"Yes, doctor."

All that Mary wanted right now was to sit down and get this over with. Stupid, inhuman regulations.

For generations, women, families, could have had as many babies as they wanted, and now... It makes you shudder. Poor little angels. They don't even know about this. Maybe it's just as well. Yes. Just as well. She nodded sadly affirming her dark thoughts.

"I understand the little angel is due in thirty two days?" The doctor's face was a study in concerned and knowledgeable fatherhood.

"Yes. Doctor." Mary whispered, as John nodded. Men never really understood these things; unless they were doctors, of course.

For a few seconds the doctor looked pensive. Then his face lightened.

"You know, you are a full month late applying for our services. But you may be lucky." He leaned over towards John. His voice assumed the confidentiality of a conspiratorial tryst. "There are always, miscarriages, you know. Very sad." Doctor's face turned very sad. "There would be, you understand, additional costs... Quite inevitable, I'm afraid. Theoretically, we are supposed to advance the patients on the waiting list. But..."

"We would be quite prepared to pay any additional expenses, doctor. Within reason, of course. We are not rich, you know."

The doctor regarded the couple with an eye of a connoisseur. Before proceeding with his offer, his mind performed a swift calculation. "Oh, my dear, dear, John. My good Sir. Who is these days? Inflation, rising taxes, and the transportation... My goodness. Who is!"

John decided to say nothing. They were late applying. One pays for ones mistakes. In more way then one. Poor Mary. She so wanted those winter holidays. They will have to wait another year. Still, at twenty-four, she had a lot of time left.

"I think, I can do it for you..." The doctor was scribbling furiously on his pad, which had been shielded from Mary and John's eyes by a raised counter. Later, the good doctor explained that the desk's shape had been so designed as to assure the confidentiality for his patients. "You wouldn't believe how low some people would stoop. I actually had a case..." There followed a very dull story all designed to inspire the Boltons' confidence in his services. "I can do it, it will be tight, mind you, for an additional eight hundred dollars."

John and Mary had little choice. It would be only four times more than they had expected. The insurance didn't cover these costs. Abortion, sure. Not suspension, though. It was not considered imperative. Eight-hundred on the top of the single payment of ten thousand. Was not a life worth that much?

"Very good, doctor." Then John hesitated. "Can you wait a little while for the full payment?"

The doctor was at his most affable. "My dear boy. Of course we shall wait. After all, we are here to help. In any way we can." With that he pressed a button.

A superb female body, only barely contained within a glued-on silk dress, entered, stopped, then proceeded forward describing perfectly symmetrical undulations with her hips. The picture perfect face atop the Miss Universe contours spoke with a voice saturated with molasses.

"Yes, doctor? What can I do for you?"

"Later. Right now, please prepare form 800/29 for Mr. and Mrs. Bolton."

The nurse *cum* private secretary, turned and left, slowly, her disarming smile lingering behind, even as her behind followed her in luxurious succession. The doctor's eyes also lingered for a little while, then found their focus on his wife's photograph, gold framed, perfunctory, on his desk. Wife with two little angels. Immediately, the good doctor was all business again.

"I shall expect you to spend the last week in our clinic. It is imperative that the little angel is prepared, before the fact as well as after, for his (it is a boy, isn't it?) temporary delay." The doctor oozed confidence. "There is absolutely nothing dangerous about the procedure, you know. You have nothing to worry about. Nothing at all."

The 'fact' was the moment of birth. The baby would be removed with a surgical procedure, which would place it in suspended animation before it took its first breath. Later, when prevailing conditions permitted, it would be resuscitated, the first breath would fill its lungs, and the 'real' birth would take place. The procedure had been tested over twenty years ago, back in '027. The results were ninety-two percent successful. The odds, worldwide, for a successful delivery were as good as a complete, or 'instant' birth, had ever been.

The door opened silently and the paragon of femininity, once again, undulated into the doctor's presence. She rested one hand on his shoulder while placing a computer printout on his desk. The doctor's face took on a healthy hue, as he held his breath until the paragon wiggled out his office. He then compensated with a few, deep gulps before returning his strained attention to his patient.

"If you just sign the standard release form, we shall set the wheels in motion. The little angel will be assured of a bright future."

No present—just future. A very distant future, thought Mary. Oh, God, how difficult can life be?

They didn't plan a third child. They knew very well it had been illegal. But how could she take upon herself to destroy him? The little innocent heart beating within her womb. A barbaric, murderous abortion? Did not her own spiritual consultant tell her that the wages of sin, a mortal sin, was eternal damnation? Eternal!

They both signed the release forms. The fee: $11,880. Ten thousand eight hundred plus 10% insurance premium in case John Bolton was unable to meet his obligations. The payments would be automatically deducted from John's future income. The interest would be calculated later. Less any amount John could scrape up as a down payment.

John did not have *anything* for the down payment. They had spent their last savings on newspaper ads, in desperate attempts to find adoptive parents for the little angel. Alas, there were none they, he and Mary, could afford. The only childless couples who were willing to adopt their third progeny were asking upwards of thirty five thousand dollars. In advance. Imagine. Almost a year's salary to adopt their wonderful child. Even if he could borrow such an exorbitant sum, in so doing, he would sentence his two children to starvation. Little Nana and Johnny III. And surely, they were his foremost obligation. Foremost. Even according to the law.

"Here is your copy of our contract. I shall expect your wife, Mrs. Bolton, to present herself in our clinic on November 3. Not a day later. If you suspect any danger of a premature delivery, call us at once. We shall make other arrangements. Remember, we are here to serve you!" With that the good doctor got up.

The interview was over.

This time, with the exception of the last slogan, the doctor's voice has been dry. The business was done. He had to get rid of them before the wife, what's her name, would start crying all over his desk. It was the usual reaction. Doctor's mind was already elsewhere. For the additional eight hundred dollars he deserved a little present. For himself. And one other person, he thought, looking at this private secretary's door. Then he glanced over his shoulder, as if expecting someone to be listening to his thoughts. In his mind's eye he saw himself at the helm of his thirty-six foot sloop, stroking the silken skin of his secretary's posterior. It was good being a doctor. One could really help people. People who needed his help. After all, he saved lives. Thousands of them. Since he enlarged the clinic to one hundred and forty beds, in a good year, tens of thousands.

It was hard, year round work, but someone had to do it. His assistants were also well compensated.

He, himself, looked after the finances. He did it rather well, he thought.

The doctor had been right about Mary Bolton's reaction. She cried all the way home. For four hours. There was nothing John could do. There was no more hope for an adoption. Anyway, they were broke. Thank God vasectomy was on Medicare. Free.

"I'll have it done tomorrow," he said, trying to cheer her up. "Really, darling. I promise. Tomorrow." He repeated. Or the day after. Soon.

She kept crying.

The cryogenic childbirth procedure had been enforced by United Nations five years after the first, successful resuscitation had been promulgated by the United Europe Research Laboratories. The scientists had already enjoyed great success with guinea pigs, rats and other rodents, for some time. The giant step had taken place in '019 when the first chimpanzee had given a protracted birth. The little beast had been removed from her mother's womb, held in suspended animation at near zero temperature, without any life supporting equipment, and resuscitated two weeks later to live happily ever after. Or at least, for as long as happy chimpanzees lived. A year later, a mature human fetus had undergone the first successful protracted birth when an expectant mother collided,

head on, with a speeding automobile. The prenatal
child had been placed in an induced hibernating
coma, maintained at low temperature for a week, and
then stimulated to regain full consciousness. That
'child' had just turned eighty-three.

The key to the success was the science of
cryogenics. Initially, it had nothing to do with
childbirth. Before the turn of the century, some labs
had experimented with the cryogenic principle in an
attempt to delay the moment of biological death of
people suffering some incurable disease. Later, the
NASA labs took up the research, in an effort to find a
way of maintaining astronauts alive, young and
healthy, during their projected trips to the near star
systems. The idea of interstellar travel became viable
in late '010, when the long predicted discovery of a
monopole led to experimentation with gravitons,
which, in turn, lead to the invention of antigravity
field, permitting local, temporary inversion of the
earth's gravity. Within four years, trips to the moon
became a popular tourist attraction.

The application of cryogenics to the protracted
birth was the direct result of the United Nations
Decree, that no one, NOBODY ON EARTH, would,
henceforth, be allowed to have more than two
children. Family planning, contraceptives and, in
spite of active opposition from a vocal minority in the

Council of Churches, the abortion was made accessible, world wide—free. It was, however, the introduction of cryogenics into the field of childbirth that placated the dissenting churches. After all, the little angels were not disposed off; the childbirth could be completed in the fullness of time—when the population of the world would finally stabilize. It was only a question of time. Or so they said. At the time.

In 2047, the churches and the mothers and fathers of not-quite-born-yet little angels were still waiting.

In 2067 John celebrated his forty-eighth birthday. Mary turned forty-four. Martha, their firstborn had just married a handsome young lad. She was twenty-three and a spitting image of her mother: five-foot-five, a naturally curly petite brunette, a docile if pensive smile on her full mouth. Her eyes were a lot less docile. They evinced serenity, forbearance, but a strong mind of her own. Like her mother. Independent.

The same year, John III, had been accepted to the World Astronautical Academy. He was a proud, dangling from his naturally broad shoulders, eighteen. At six-one, as tall as his father, lanky, easy going but simultaneously, if surprisingly, very ambitious. These days one had to be. Or—live in perpetual boredom on a Federal subsidy. Three years later, at twenty-one, he looked terrific in his second lieutenant's, pure white, uniform. The blue, naval insignia matched perfectly the color of his eyes.

The little angels slept.

That same year, in '070, World Federation of Nations had been forced to make a drastic decision. The world population continued to rise, slowly. Nevertheless, it did rise. People refused to die. It had been one thing to legislate temporary suspended animation, quite another to tell people to drop dead. Even for common good. As a direct result of magnificent progress in bioengineering, life expectancy had increased to 124 and 131 for men and women, respectively. And even then, after all these years, there were some nations that refused to obey to decree of the United Nations, issued some twenty-five years ago. The world population kept rising. At nine-point-seven billion, the earth was bursting in her seams.

There was one other problem.

The Little Angels Franchises Inc. reported that they were running out of space for storage of the... little angels. Alaska, Greenland, Siberia, parts of the Northern Territories of Canada, and even the two, half-melted, polar caps were solid with little boxes of ice, each protecting the precious half-life of a mature fetus. The question was, what to do with the still growing number of illegal pregnancies.

The periodic religious revivals persuaded some people to refuse the use of contraceptive devices. An even greater number thought twice before undergoing an abortion. In addition, the bioengineering innovations had rekindled the macho spirit in men. They thought three times before undergoing a vasectomy. At forty-eight, John Bolton looked more mature rather than older. He could perform greater feats of physical strength and endurance than he did twenty years ago. And he was not alone.

The World Council authorized the installation of Little Angels Inc. storage depots on the moon. The possibility of the use of other orbiting depots had been discussed. Five years later, at night, one could see four satellites orbiting the earth with nine month old, half-born children. The half-mile diameter frozen globes looked quite pretty. They testified to man's superiority over animals. We did not kill our children.

At forty-three, Martha Ying Tan, nee Bolton, had undergone a protracted birth procedure. It was her seventh. Her husband Mao, was a young fifty-two year old, who did his body-building exercises daily. He had bought some stock in Little Angels Inc. on the Pacific Stock exchange a long time ago. The shares had split seven times since he bought them. They also paid the highest dividends. He could well afford to remain macho.

The problems really started in late 2087.

The polar icecaps began melting in earnest about a year earlier. No one knew for sure what had caused the sudden rise in global temperature. The scientists talked about some greenhouse effects, for at least a century, and nothing happened. After the first fifty years people simply ignored the pessimistic prophets. The back-to-nature trend was no longer fashionable.

Then the decision had been made to complete the birth cycle for all the little angels who were in any danger of suffering irreparable damage. Within a year, the number of revived babies soared to five hundred and sixty million. A year later, the number passed the one billion mark. The Little Angels Inc. shares plunged headlong into the Pacific ocean. Mass suicides helped to counteract the expanding population a little, but not enough.

A decision had to be made.

"The voting is tomorrow. Have you made up your mind?" John asked Mary. At sixty-eight he was active in all walks of life. He looked and felt young. In many ways, he was.

"Do we have any choice?"

Mary had long lost interest in the messes created by all levels of the government. As far back as the seventies, the leaders had lost the art of covering up their mistakes. They lost the knack of pass-the-buckmanship. People refused the buck. The governing bodies resorted to referenda. Mary no longer cared. She spent her time painting. Her acrylics were recognized as a good investment. To her, their monetary value was of little interest.

"Well, they are afraid to make the decision themselves. As usual. That is why they organized a referendum. So, we do have a choice." John explained.

"I didn't mean that."

"I know..."

Mary did not mean whether they had a choice between a ney or yea vote. She meant, what would happen if the majority would be against the immediate placing of the new born babies in deep hibernation. Such a vote would solve the temperature rise problem, but it required a life support system. Albeit, a rudimentary one, but it had to be paid for. By the people. As usual.

"Well?" John asked.

"If I were you, I would sell your stock in the Little Angels and buy the Life Support Systems shares on the Trans Pacific. I would do it now."

John dialed the Stock Exchange on his laptop. The LitAng dropped almost three hundred points since last year. It was still worth about ten times what he paid for it. He sighed.

"What are you waiting for?" Mary asked. Frankly, she didn't give a damn about money. She derived joy from her creativity. Even if she hadn't been able to sell any of her paintings, she would have continued to work on her chosen art form. She believed that creativity was the essence of life. Also, ever since she had had to subject her body to Dr. Angles ministrations, she hated procrastination.

While John waited, the LitAng dropped another two points. John dialed his personal code and the sell instruction. Immediately his automatic printout indicated his new credit. He converted it at once to The LifeSS stock. By the end of the day, he had doubled his money. It seemed that he, or rather Mary had guessed right.

They both voted on the Yea side. The waken babies would go back to sleep. What else could they have done? And anyway, babies enjoyed sleeping. Everyone knew that.

Only that was not the end of it.

In '87, the problem may have been amusing—to

some. Progressively it worsened. It really stopped being funny about three years later. The number of little angels being brought to life had passed the five billion mark. Brought to life and immediately put to sleep. Deep relaxing coma. As deep a sleep as one can be in, without actually dying. Nevertheless, it was sleep. The babies were really alive. And that was the rub.

The difference between the two states created the fundamental problem. The frozen fetuses were not alive. They were and they weren't. They were alive in the sense that they were not dead. But there had not been any brain activity that even the most delicate electroencephalogram could have measured. At the same time, they could not have been dead, simply because they were never fully born. They were alive in the sense that your nails or hair are alive. Not any more. Some said, a lot less.

But by the time the birth cycle had been completed, the babies were officially born. One could actually measure minute electrical brain discharges. The thoughts generated may have been in the deepest of the subconscious, but they were there. The babies were definitely alive.

By '93, the number of dormant babies had swollen to nine billion. They had no choice. The climate made the conditions of Little Angels depots too risky. Too risky to the little angels' lives. The Boltons voted for total conversion.

"We must play it safe," John insisted. "After all, one of them could be ours..."

His stock went through the roof. He could now convert to real estate and retire.

"Retire at seventy-four? Don't be silly, John. You are a young man. You have practically a whole life in front of you." Mary insisted.

They took a two months trip to Mars to think about it. Why not? They always wanted to travel. For quite a while they couldn't afford it. Now they could. Thanks to the green house effect. If that's what it was.

Since the babies now counted in the official census of the Federated Republics, the total population of the planet earth now boasted a shade under eighteen billion. That's not counting the Moon Base, some colonies on Mars and the geodesic structures in the asteroid belt. Some said it was too much. Half the future voters, slept. Government was trying to legislate them as proxies.

And then all hell broke loose.

John had noticed the first signs of trouble the day

after they got back from Mars. The trip was the most boring two months they had ever spent in their life. Cooked up in a box, to emerge on the other side into another box, and then, back again. Their trips to the Moon in fully glazed cruisers were a lot more exciting. Anyway, the trouble was in the air. Or, perhaps, the cable?

The TV morning news (had it been evening news, it would have given John nightmares) reported that some ghostly apparitions demanding that they give up their souls had visited a number of people. These initial reports, however, had been dismissed as a natural result ensuing from the United Earth Federation celebrations, commemorating the day, when the remaining, diehard republics had joined the Federation. The following two days, the reports of apparitions have increased in number. It was becoming increasingly difficult to define the visions of thousands petrified people as an extended hangover ensuing from the celebrations. Then, unavoidably, the United Churches Council got into the act. The Council announced: The end of the world. At hand, of course.

That's fine, said the citizenry, but what do we do in the meantime?

"Pray!" said the Council.

"To whom, for what, and how?" replied the

willing congregations. The old prayer systems had proven fairly unreliable. And, by then, there were so many religions that it was quite difficult, near impossible, to select a god who might have any interest in the ghostly apparitions, let alone other man's problems.

And then the sightings began in earnest.

Every day, or night really, just about every person, male or female had been approached, mostly during his or her sleep, with insistent demands that they relinquish their souls. There had been threats, although no one fully understood them, threats of 'mental violence' or of 'emotional upheavals', or, even more crazy, of 'zombification'. Honest. Zombification was the word used in a number of news reports.

John and Mary took the matters relatively calmly. They had long learned to take the unexpected in their stride. This, however, caught them lying down. It had not been easy.

"What the devil do you think it is? Some mental aberration resulting from changes in climatic conditions?"

John had long learned to pose the difficult questions to Mary rather then try to fathom them himself. Mary had an unholy, or perhaps a blessed, ability to see through the haze of circumstances and cut directly to the heart of the matter.

"It's pretty obvious." She said calmly, adding a few more deft stokes on her canvas.

"Obvious?" Normally, on such occasions, John waited until Mary was good and ready to supply the answer. This time, though, it was too much. John was a little rattled. "Obvious!?"

Mary finished painting, swirled her brush in a water container, wiped it clean with calm deliberation, then turned her attention to her husband. Her face did not give away anything. John often thought that she had learned to display this inscrutable expression from her son-in-law. After all, the Chinese were the recognized masters of poker face.

"John, what is the ancient, recognized difference between man and animal?" she asked.

"I was under an impression that man is an animal," he contested.

"That is quite true. But is that all he is?"

John wanted to say: "Of course not". But he caught himself in the nick of time. If man is not only an animal, than what else is he?

"You tell me," he challenged. The last hundred arguments, on subjects that bordered on the metaphysical, he'd lost. He didn't feel like loosing again. And this subject carried distinct metaphysical overtones.

"All right. I will tell you." Mary remained sitting on her stool. Her back straight, her chin up as if looking over some object. John never understood how she could remain comfortable in this position for hours on end. "There are eighteen billion bodies on earth and nine billion souls which enjoy free will. Something's got to give."

John wanted to ask her if she had been drinking. He thought better of it.

"You're serious...?"

"Can you think of a better explanation? For as long as the bodies had been frozen, there was nothing to differentiate between them and the bodies of any animals. Then, we screwed up the climate. After all, we had been warned about it for about a hundred years. Nature is a very patient lady. But never mind that. The moment the bodies were brought to life, the brain, the glandular system, the dream awareness had all come into being. When you sleep, you are still alive, aren't you? You do not claim to become an animal in bed—although in your case that's a bad comparison. Anyway, you continue to be human..."

"So what has my sex life got to do with the sleeping babies?" John interrupted.

"So it appears that time has come for us all to pay the piper. We used up our allotted period in our bodies. It's time someone else had a go at living. At becoming. The Earth, the air, the food, even the oceans are finite. Why not the number of souls?" Mary mused.

"You've got to be kidding...."

Whatever he wanted to say he didn't finish. The air seemed to vibrate all around him. The room, the furniture, even Mary, directly in front to him, lost the sharpness of her contour definition. It was as if John was looking at the energy that everything projected, rather then at the object itself.

Then a hazy, shimmering pattern emerged, from nowhere, in the middle of the room. The phantom solidified to be at least as solid as everything else at this moment.

"Good God!" John pressed his shoulders into the back of the armchair. "For crying out loud, can't you see it?"

"See what darling?" Mary asked calmly.

"The, the... what is it?" John screamed. He could scream as well as any woman. After the last laryngitis he had a bionic throat put in.

Mary returned to her painting.

"Oh, really John," she smiled. "Are you trying to scare me?"

The air around John reverted to normal. He swallowed hard. He saw it and he heard it. Whatever the bloody thing was. It was as scary as anything he had ever seen. Although, he had no idea why. It was just like what the people on the news programs had said.

"You must learn to relax more, John. You will do yourself harm screaming like that." Mary added some ochre to the foreground of her canvas. She forgot about his bionic larynx.

"I tell you, I saw it," he said at last.

"Of course you did," she agreed calmly.

"Then what the hell am I supposed to do about it?" He almost screamed again.

"Get used to it."

"What?"

"John. We have all placed the little angels in deep coma. It is a well known, proven, medical fact, that in the coma condition one is apt to suffer most terrible nightmares. The psychologists warned us against this step at the time. Something to do with archetypal memories. As usual, we ignored the warnings."

"So is that supposed to make me feel better?"

"So the little angels are attempting, in any way they can, to get out of their dilemma. They seem to have some control of—what we can only call—their mental and emotional bodies, and they demand to be given full awareness. Perhaps a soul, they seem to refer to so much, is the state, or condition, or a body of full awareness. Perhaps we should learn to share our souls with them."

"How the devil can I do that?" John was close to a nervous breakdown.

"Relax. Next time you have a 'vision', don't panic."

"It's easy for you to say. You don't see any apparitions," he grumbled.

Mary put down her brush again. She turned to John, a deep serenity, perhaps even happiness shimmering in her awe-filled eyes.

"Don't I? Perhaps I just happen to remember, that it could be my own son."

John gave up. This had nothing to do with any ghosts, yet he never did win a single argument, which even remotely bordered on the twilight zone. Also, he suffered from shock and, right now, felt quite despondent.

On the way to the liquor cabinet he passed behind Mary's easel. The canvas she was working was a large one. About four feet by three. In the foreground was a very young image of their son Johnny. At first sight, Johnny's face seemed almost expressionless. Then, the large, empty, round eyes, and equally round, open mouth became frozen in a silent, evocative cry. Tiny, baby-like arms reached out, as though imploring his father to help. This was not a portrait of Johnny, but the likeness was quite unmistakable. The body of the little lad was shrouded by a shimmering, spectral mist.

Behind Johnny, there were other faces. Many, many faces. As John looked closer, their features seemed quite old, yet in a strange way, also baby-like. They all resembled their Johnny. The procession of faces, framed by the pudgy arms with grasping, chubby, little fingers, stretched into infinity.

Mary, a wistful smile hovering at the corners of her mouth, resumed painting.

***

Open Casket

I felt considerably out of place. Not that I objected to paying last respects to someone who had no idea I was doing it, but still, habits last a long time. We all do it. We wait until somebody leaves this valley of tears before we decide that, instead of criticizing them we should shower respects on them. Men or women. We're all alike. Phonies.

Or perhaps we do so because we feel guilty?

No matter.

My problem was that I had no idea why I was here. I was drifting along without a care in the world and then, suddenly, I found myself sitting in the first row of a chapel, looking at an open casket. All around me, and I knew this without turning my head, were people with somber expressions on their faces, occasionally glancing at their watches. I felt like taking a nap, only, for some reason, my eyes wouldn't close. Actually they did, but it didn't seem like it. My awareness of my surroundings remain the same.

I shrugged by shoulders and decided to bear the occasion with the others. Some twenty others. Actually, most people I knew. I mean, I know. There was George and Sally, my long time friends. Also…

Suddenly it came to me that I had no idea who was taking an eternal rest in the casket. An expensive looking coffin, with frills and embroidery.

What a waste, I mused. The poor bastard inside didn't give a damn. Bastard? It could have been a bastardess, or whatever the female of a bastard is. An illegitimate something or other.

Actually he or she might have been very nice people. I had no idea who he or she was. Had been. In fact, I had no idea what the devil I was doing here. I opened by eyes and here I was. A week ago I was flying to a meeting in Paris, first class I might add (the firm was paying). Then things got a bit murky. I must have dozed off or something. Anyway, here I was, sitting still, trying to look somber and respectful. I was really curious who it was.

Then I remembered Paris.

It was beautiful. I remember strolling *Avenue des Champs-Élysées* last Sunday, all the way from *Clemenceau* metro station to the *Arc de Triomphe*, a must for any visitor to Paris. I gazed as much at the trees aligning both sides as I did at the abundance of *demoiselles* flaunting the latest Parisian modes. Perhaps that is why I had little recollection of anything else. I seemed attuned to recall only the nice, the pleasant, the beautiful flashes in my life.

Ah oui, there was also a meeting about something…

And then things got murky.

I have no recollection of flying back. I remember boarding the plane, downing a vodka-Martini, putting on earphones and then...

And then a gray cloud obscured my vision. I must have fallen asleep.

And now, here I am sitting at someone's Open Casket Funeral. I was never one for such morbid ceremonies. You live then you die, and with luck, if the mystics are right, you live again in a new body.

I stole a glance to my left and nearly gave up *my* ghost. Dressed all in black, a black veil over her face, a hanky in her hand, was — you wont believe it — was my wife.

My own, beautiful, loving wife!

I closed my eyes, blinked a few times, and sneaked another glance. Yea, it was Doris. It was she, all right. But if she was here why wasn't I invited.

Stupid?

I must have been! I'm here, aren't I?

I simulated an attack of cough and turned to my left, right, and partially behind me. There were a number of my friends. About twenty of them. Some I haven't seen for quite a while. What the hell were they all doing here?

My parents were both dearly departed, as were my wife's. We had no children. Who was the blighter in the casket?

Obviously whoever it was must have share our friends. I suddenly realized that all I need do is to find out who was missing. Who was recently departed. It if hadn't been for my Paris trip I would have known.

A padre took his stance and started talking. All nice things were said by him and a couple of other people. The guy who died, I knew it was a guy by now, must have been a pretty nice guy. They spoke about his as though I knew him myself. Yea, a really nice guy.

And then we all got up to file past the coffin. I was glad it would soon be over. I offered by arm to my wife, but, for some reason she ignored it. Have I offended her?

The problem was that my memory was hazy from about the time I fell asleep in the plane.

Damn it. Something must have happened. They must have put something in my Martini. Or I must have hit my head on something.

Why can't I remember???

I walked three paces behind my wife. She stopped by the corpse and whispered something I couldn't hear. I hoped she wasn't swearing. If she and I were sitting in the front raw, it must have been someone close to us. Uncle Joe? Cousin Mavis, she was in her eighties…

Or… it must be Frank, my brother from my father's first marriage. He lived only some fifty miles away, and probably wanted to be buried in the same cemetery as the rest of the family. I wasn't into that sort of thing. When you're gone, you're gone, I always thought. Who cares when they bury the carcass. It wouldn't be of any use to me any more.

Let the worms have a feast…

My wife wiped her eyes for the third time and moved on. It was time for me to solve the mystery of the corpse. At first glance, he looked like a good looking fellow.

And then I stood still.

I mean really still.

Frozen still.

I was looking down at a beautifully made up image of my face. I never looked that good. Not for the last ten years or so. I looked closer. It wasn't my face at all. It was a great mask. Obviously made by a talented artist.

At the next moment an image flashed before my eyes. The roar of the engine emitted a few hiccups and then we were inside of a ball of fire. That explained the mask. My face must have burned to a crisp. Probably the blue suit was stuffed to look like a human body.

So why open coffin?

And then I remembered. Our home was lined with dozens of masks plastered all over the walls. My wife's specialty. She was a very talented sculptress. Her 'faces' adorned our Town Hall with all past mayors' visages. The mask was the very last gift she had given me.

Posthumously.

Just lucky, I suppose. Last year she made me promise that we would have an open coffin funeral. She said she'd make sure no one would see my ugly face. I hoped they'd remove the mask before they buried the coffin. As I was saying, I never looked that good.

Darling Doris. She was always a giver. Even now.

The memory dissolved in a cacophony of fire engines rushing to the scene. I smiled. I didn't care.

I wasn't there any more.

***

The Next Step

It's been many millennia since I trod the hard dust under my feet. Being human had its good points but needing clothing, housing, eternal struggle to get food... and then the jealousies that developed between the haves and the have-nots drove me to near-despair.

We never run out of food. It's like living inside a refrigerator. Nice, and cool, and plenty of food. Always.

And then there were the leaders.

Those among them who were by far the most inept ones, who did not or could not find anything creative to do for the good of all, insisted on telling others what to do.

And also there were the military maniacs. They proclaimed *"thou shalt not kill"* maxims, only to murder every one who disagreed with them. With their concept of fair play, wherein the rich must get richer at the expense of the poor. They would attack other humans just to get more of what they already had too much. The strange commodity they hunger so much is money. They can't eat it, play with it, put it to any practical use, other than exchanging it for something they have too much of already.

How stupid can you get?

I recall the newcomers.

Only last month a fellow arrived to join us. They thought he was dead and burned his body. Of course he left it at the last moment. Not surprisingly, having lost both legs and one arm by stepping on a mine buried on a village road, he wouldn't have enjoyed staying in it.

Can you imagine it? Burying mines on village roads? What sort of mind can develop such perfidy. Such utter depravity. Only humans can sink so low.

Ha, ha…

I could sink much, much lower than humans! And loving it! Although, most of the time, I preferred shallower grounds. But that's just me. Some of my cousins like it both, cool and deep. After all, there is plenty of room for all of us. Seventy percent of Earth's surface is water-covered, and, although I have visited some rivers, just out of curiosity, ninety-six percent of water is in the ocean.

And we had a lovely group. Several hundred.

We had such fun!

With little need for hunting, echolocation took care of that, we had lot of time to play around. Leaping out of water to spy-hop to view our surroundings, bow-riding ships to conserve energy, or just dancing by synchronizing our movements with one another. It seems that we spent must of our lives just having fun.

And then there were the humans.

Imagine, 7.5 billion people on just thirty percent of the Earth dry surface. No wonder they are fighting for every square inch. I vaguely remember how crowded it was. And we are under a million. Room for everybody. And our 'room' is three-dimensional.

If it were up to me, I'd have stayed in my domain for ever. Or even longer. Ha, ha!

Of course, not everybody is allowed to join us. You have to reach a certain level of intelligence. We don't blame the humans. With their 16,000,000,000 neurons compared to our 37,200,000,000, it is hardly their fault. But it's not just the equipment they have, but their ability use it. Without the constant cooling effect of water our brains would boil over. Imagine, all the synapses firing at once!

But they don't.

Why?

Because we're not stupid.

Also, we don't live on land.

Ha, ha, ha!

Idiots?

Actually not idiots. Just primitives. I know. I used to be one of them. Years and years and years ago. In my kindergarten.

Poor guys. And they all think they are the super-species

Ha, ha, ha again!

And talking of species, there are some thirty-eight of ours, more living in the rivers. Imagine if humans had thirty-eight races, let alone species, each of a different colour. Wouldn't that be fun? Their racism would explode heavens high. Everybody would hate everybody. Full time. They would have little time left to do anything else.

And when all the fun is over there is the mating season. For most of us it's throughout the year. Some of us prefer spring and fall. Why? I have no idea. Ask them.

As soon as a baby is born, mother takes it to the surface so it can take its first breath. The child will stay with the mother until its three to eight years old. We're all different. Some learn faster than others, but at eight we're mature enough to take care of ourselves. Of course we don't have crime or speeding vehicles to endanger them.

Most people have to die to go to heaven. We are already there. We are in heaven. We are surrounded by beauty that humans have never seen. But its here. It's paradise. A veritable garden of Eden.

So why am I telling you all this?

For me, there was only one problem.

Joan.

I've known her 3 reincarnations. She was almost ready to make the jump to our paradise. To vacate her body and join us. In the last moment she got scared. Someone joked that she'd lose her beautiful hair. From time immemorial some people were obsessed with their hair. Remember Samson?

Anyway, you know women. Hair is their crowning glory. And Joan was very much a woman.

Very, very much a woman.

When she joined us, for a while she tried growing her hair. After all a strong mind and a passionate desire can create anything. Even miracles. Around that time people began talking about sightings of sirens. Joan had friends. Beautiful ladies with beautiful, long hair.

And, did I mention?

She had a beautiful voice. A mezzo-contralto. It was like honey being poured into your ears. People said it was hypnotic. Mesmerizing.

But then she got cold feet. Did I mention she still had her feet? Joined together they looked like a tail. A fishtail.

Then, one day, she woke up below and took a deep breath. It was her last in her new body. She didn't know that newcomers to our species must take their first breaths of air above water. For quite a while. Like babies.

She also forgot that to prevent drowning while sleeping, only half of our brain goes to sleep, while the other half stays awake, so that we can continue to breathe.

To bad.

The next day she woke up in a human form. I was hoping that she'd come back. Soon. I even prayed.

I missed her.

A lot.

After a long while the pain got too much.

So, I had little choice. After a few millennia in the glorious kingdom of the oceans, I went back on dry land. Most people believe in reincarnation. This is different. They call it transmigration. Usually people move forward, or at least walk in vicious circles. But not me. I needed my Joan the way a dolphin needs water.

She was my life.

Anyway. After all this time... The word millennia is meaningless. It only applies in the reality men invented because they couldn't understand the concept of time. Only now matters. The Now with a capital N. All else is imaginary.

Nevertheless, after a few millennia in the more advanced reality, we didn't fall in love with the body of a woman, or man, for that mater. We fall in love with what made them the way they are. The way they became because of what they are. The outside is only the cover. Like cover of a book. But what we really love in the story, not the book cover.

In a way, we are all love stories.

Still, I hope, one day, one century or millennium, she'll give up her hair and we shall both return to the kingdom of water. There, and only there we can communicate telepathically. It gives us a sense of oneness. Of unity. Isn't this what love really is? Being One?

And there we had been one. In the vastness of the oceans.

There and only there we could move up and down and laterally without any polluting, noisy gadgets.

Only there we are not limited to language, or a country, or polluted air, or climate, or obsessed with "things".

Only there we are free as angels.

As gods?

***

George did not feel well.

Again.

It's been four years since they went out, together, to share the gold, the red, the stale yet ever congenial, intimate fragrance of autumn leaves. Now, there were hardly any leaves left. A lone pine, a spruce, a clamp of firs, stood out boldly against the perpetually gray, indifferent, melancholy sky. The few remaining conifers, mostly stained brown, reminded them of the sea of green. A sea turned dull, the color of an overripe olive, soon to be wrapped in a uniform, dispassionate blanket, depersonalized, stored for yet another season. And, she remembered, it was hot. Stiflingly, pressingly hot.

Jean wondered if she and George would share the spring thaw. The last few years they counted the days from the first snow, marking them off on a wall calendar in the kitchen, till the first, audacious snowdrop would poke its head, curiously, through the dark grey, filthy slime of residual winter. They would see them with their binoculars. Down below. Thank God, winters were so much shorter these days.

The grey city slush had little in common with its distant cousin in the once open, inviting countryside. There, the first snow settled gently on the awaiting grass; the blades spread apart, as though with open arms welcoming the season of rest, of calm, hibernation. Out there, then, nature had not objected to the winter season. Not even human nature. Not until old age became nervous, afraid to miss even a few weeks of what passed, nowadays, for living. From being just that little less sedentary, a little less cold—a chill in the bones—no matter how many sweaters and blankets and degrees on the thermostat they used to cover the fragile, aching body, equally demanding of rest as of hope, of spring, so distant, so very distant.

Jean remembered well their weekends in the country. Even after they no longer went skiing with the children. There had been the daily walks in the crisp, country air, the crunching of fresh snow under their, still useful, *àpres ski* boots. The cotton wool, puffy whiteness, poised sometimes gently, sometimes quite heavily, on the outer reaches of the soon-to-be Christmas trees, shimmering, sparkling. They walked arm in arm, interlocked in a lifetime of memories, of shared beauty, happiness, sorrow, but always shared, now slowly covered by a creeping, snarling blanket of forgetfulness.

"It's time to wake up, George. We must try to stay awake, awhile. Must keep up our strength."

This morning, as Jean made coffee for breakfast, George marked up yesterday's square on the calendar. He then stood a long time studying the pages full of numbers, many, many numbers, black, red on Sundays, more than he could count, stretching into the future. Afterwards, he did not feel well, again. The springtime was much too far away.

"Why?" George opened his eyes, slightly red. He wiped a tear perpetually forming in the corner of his left eye.

He slept an awful lot lately. Ten hours during the night, then another two or so during the morning, and three, sometimes four, during the afternoon soap operas—the old reruns, the same over the last four years. Jean wondered what was better. To weave his own dreams, or to listen and watch others do it. Perhaps he was right. Perhaps one shouldn't fight the natural course of nature. But if They see the shape he is in...?

"I need your help. I can't cope with this..."

Or with that, or the other. This was the one thing that always got George up and coming. It motivated him to make an extra effort. If Jean asked him to help. She lied. She invented the chores. Jean was as independent as one could be within a spherical homestead. There had been but one reason why she'd never mastered the art of true independence. She needed to be needed. She needed George a lot more than George needed her. All her life she has been, and now continued to be, a mother. What else could she have done? Her four children, scattered halfway across the galaxy—who knew where, exactly—have long flown the domestic coop. They couldn't stay to look after their parents. They had traded convenience and security for true independence. But what choice did Jean have? Jean, and so many others?

When the opportunity presented itself, they all went for the homestead. All who had been at least over sixty, then, mostly over sixty-five. The others had left, some died, futilely, inconsequentially trying. Trying what? To fight the invisible? In those days, those had been difficult choices: to die living, or to live—slowly dying. Or, so it seemed, at the time. It was different now. Time heals, builds up a scab over the wound. Forgives.

A homestead had been offered to all who made

their choice to stay. There had been no pressure. No special incentives. Just a generous offer. No strings. Practically. The spheroid house offered all the latest conveniences. A lot more than Jean had been used to. And it did give her the feeling of security that she would be able to look after George, for as long as it took. These days, with the walks in the country belonging to distant, cherished memories, she chose not to take advantages of some of the labour saving devices the homestead offered. She too needed to keep moving. To keep fit. To be able to look after her George. Who else would?

A funny name "homestead". No land, no outbuildings, no generations to give it roots, history. Just three levels. Machinery at the bottom, living, working—whatever—in the middle, and the garden above. All within a sphere. Enclosed, protected. Quite neat, really.

On the outside, the homesteads looked a lot more attractive than many prefabs she had seen during her lifetime. True, they were all identical, but so were many houses, put up by developers, long before the offer came. In fact the spheres, on occasion, or viewed from a certain angle, were almost invisible. They were polished on the outside, and that made them practically disappear. Except for the distortion, of course. But who could complain about distortion?

Was not this whole world quaintly distorted Had it been her fault? Or the fault of the countless billions of her predecessors? The previous generations? Years after years, till it became too late. A point of no return. At least, not for fifty years. So They said.

Jean remembered, her mother, dear mother, had shown her pictures of glass domes. Jean could not have been more than ten or twelve then... Her mother had said that Buckminster Fuller had designed the spheres. A Gentle Giant, she had called him. Geodesic structures. An omen? They were meant to help man solve the housing problem.

So many years ago...

Now, the homesteads, offered a closed system. Ecologically complete. Efficient. In many ways, one could say, perfect. Only no one said so. There had been, there was, something missing. That is why the young ones left. They just couldn't take it. There are so many things you can't take when you are young. So many things...

George went to sleep again.

Lucky they were not reporting tonight. They had to. Once a week. It was, really, for their own good. The tenants could ask for certain items of particular interest. Like some old video tapes. They always obliged. They really were very nice. They did the

best They could. It's just that Jean was afraid that if
They saw George's condition, They might insist on
some medical attention. Somewhere away from their
own homestead. Who would she look after then? She
knew that George did not want to be moved. Ever.
He said so many times. Many times. But if he
continued sleeping, they might not tolerate it. She
didn't know for sure, but people talked. People
always talked, no matter how much they were given.
They wanted more. They complained. Jean didn't.

She remembered the last time, when Johnny and
Brenda came to see them, just before shipping out to
the colonies. The twins left months earlier. Brenda,
the youngest, her hair ever disheveled, even on a
perfectly calm day; Johnny tall, almost robust, firm,
adamant determination etched in his, oh, so very blue
eyes. They both were so full of life. Not she and
George—the children. The prospect of facing the
uncertain, of breaching the rough, the unknown, did
not in any way scare them. They were not even
nervous.

"We are shipping tomorrow. We came to say
goodbye, mother."

Goodbye? Was it again like her own great-great-
grandfather who took a boat across the ocean never to
be seen again? Then, there may had been letters. But
now? How do you send a letter across a million

million kilometers of the dark void of space? The pigeons didn't fly that far. The pigeons didn't fly at all. The pigeons were long dead.

What do you say to your own child whom, in all likelihood, you would never see again? Never is such a long time. So very long.

"I love you, darling. I love you so very, very much..."

Five thousand million mothers saying goodbye to five thousand million sons and daughters. Fathers standing by, chin thrust forward, a stiff upper lip denying a smile of encouragement, shoulders squared, those few who could still square them.

It had been that or the homestead. The young ones didn't really have any choice.

"George, will you help me with supper? I need the potatoes peeled."

Jean never told George that they had a food synthesizer. She could press the button and, seconds later, the meal would come out. The potatoes he peeled were also synthetic. He never noticed. At least he peeled them. He kept busy. His fingers got some exercise. "I must get him upstairs, into the garden". He did so love gardening, once. Complained he hardly ever had a chance.

George got up, went to the bathroom, emerged

fifteen minutes later and sat down, again, on the long, extended lounge chair. His favourite place for a protracted nap. All his naps were protracted. He forgot why he'd gotten up in the first place. It must have been to go to the bathroom.

"George, the potatoes...?"

"What, dear? The potatoes? No, thanks, I don't think I shall have any. Not hungry."

Jean knew George didn't recognize a meal to be a proper meal unless it was served with potatoes. Eighty-seven years is a long time to form a habit.

"That's all right, George. But could you prepare some for me?"

"What's that? For you, dear? Oh, yes. I am coming. I'll just take a little nap and I shall be right with you." It didn't work, this time.

George had just slept two hours.

They told them that in about fifty, sixty years, their children could come back to earth. From the colonies—if they survived them. The air should be acceptable by then. The water potable. The vegetables would not burn their throats with acid, the fish would not poison their livers or kidneys. All the remedial chemicals had been spread, throughout the globe, from the air. The rest, the earth, nature, had to do herself. She would purify herself. She simply needed time. About fifty years. Forty-six years to go. Forty-six years is a very long time when you are eighty-four years old. And tired. Sometimes—so very, very tired.

They say the snow in fifty years will be white, even in the city. Except that there would not be a city. The homesteads could be placed anywhere in the country. They were supported on telescopic tripods. No foundations were required. Each of the three legs could be extended to an incredible length, until it found resistance enough to support the sphere. The homestead could be set on land, or water, or in the Rocky Mountains. If the supports did not find sufficient bearing capacity, the sphere would simply float to a different location. The system was fully automatic. And foolproof. So They said.

Jean gave up on the potatoes. She allowed George to sleep. Once, he had been so active. She had to hold him back—way back when. "You must take care of yourself," she used to tell him. "You have to last a long time."

He didn't.

The supper was ready. George had to get up, now. She had set up the table upstairs, on the domed, garden patio. There was quite a nice view, from up there. If you ignored the grayness. Mist mixed with the airborne pollution. They couldn't do anything about that. That was part of the heritage. Only time could take care of that.

Jean remembered the day the Brothers had made the announcement. They offered help. They did not force their presence on anyone. They said, that sentient beings always made their own choices. It was a question of balance. Freedom and responsibility. Inseparable. The last few generations of man had too much freedom.

They offered a choice. Anyone who wanted to, could be transported to other planets. Primitive planets, rather like the earth had been, perhaps, half a million years ago. Virgin planets. Unspoiled. No pollution. They would be given all the necessary help to set up an agrarian society. They would be given a fresh start. Imagine. They said it would take seven different planets to support the population of the earth if ecological balance were to be maintained.

Only five planets were, in fact, necessary. The older people preferred to die in their own backyard. "You shouldn't transplant old mushrooms," Jean remembered her own grandmother saying. She and George had decided to stay. All those who had chosen to stay, have been placed in homesteads. They simply woke up, one day, inside the large transparent spheres. They had no idea how they got there. Even when the children came to say goodbye, they came through, what they called, a "transporter". It was a cabinet, like an old-fashioned shower stall. You had to know the coordinates. If you didn't, you could end up in the middle of the ocean. Or underground. Or half a mile up, on a grey, putrid cloud. They were given the coordinates at the Central Processing Station. They left for the virgin planets from there. In groups, or individually. The sentient beings always had a choice.

The central processing sphere, Johnny said, was so large you couldn't see the other end. It hung only about four hundred meters, or so, above the ground. It just stood there. Hovered, really. The funny thing was, it didn't cast any shadow, Johnny insisted. When it first appeared, for a while, no one had noticed it. In spite of its size. Then the Pentagon wanted to test the resilience of the shimmering, polished walls with their rockets. Something to do with sovereign territory. Whatever happened to sovereign hospitality? The rockets failed to explode. They simply disintegrated, rather like a snowball made from too dry snow. There was no debris under the sphere from the unexploded shells. Just nothing. It seemed that the rocket must have entered the dome and failed to come out on the other end. It didn't make any sense. The Russians offered help with their transcontinental ballistic missiles. They fired about a dozen of them with the Presidential approval. Again nothing happened. They couldn't use the H bombs, of course. It would have been suicidal. More than a year had passed, and the sphere just hung there. It did not move an inch, as though it were anchored to the rock underneath. Only it wasn't.

On the four hundred and thirty fifth day after its arrival, or after the appearance of the sphere out of nowhere, They made the announcement. All the airways, the radio, the television, the secret, big business or army intercoms—whatever—they all broadcast exactly the same message. Every single country, throughout the world, heard the message in their own language. Sometimes, people heard two or three languages while listening in the same room. Strange?

They called themselves the Brothers. Just that, Brothers. They said that if the greenhouse effect is allowed to continue, the melting of the remainder of the polar snow and icecap would not only result in global inundations, but it would, will They said, cause the earth axis to tilt substantially. Before the new earth axis could stabilize itself, there would be geological adjustments in the tectonic plates. This, in turn, would result in wide spread volcanic activity. They said that a minimum of ninety percent of the earth population would die in the resulting cataclysms. Perhaps more.

They couldn't be sure.

Then, following the announcement, there had been silence for three weeks. Washington, Moscow, Peking, and Berlin issued a joint communiqué, advising the "Brothers", quite politely, to mind their own business. The communiqué said thank you, but no thank you. It said that the human race is well capable of taking care of its own. There had been no response to the joint communiqué.

Precisely twenty-one days after the original broadcast, little, or not so little, globes, about forty feet in diameter, began appearing in different parts of the world. It looked as if the enormous sphere had been having babies. The spheres, shimmering little globes, were the homesteads. Homes for those who did not want, or could not, take advantage of the other offer. The offer of starting from scratch. Elsewhere.

About one billion decided to stay. Five hundred million domes. All identical. A couple to a dome. Could be more, up to four people. People too old, or too sick, or too lazy, to go. Jean and George amongst them. Not lazy. Could anyone blame them? The Brothers didn't.

They were lucky that evening. It must have turned colder. For the first time in four month, they could see a misty, deep red sunset. George looked up from his plate. His face was awash with crimson twilight. The red reflected in his eyes, rather like cat's eyes. He smiled.

"It must be late autumn," he said. "I remember this colour. We were up north, it was a month after the Mount Royal erupted. The sunset had the same colour."

That must have been eleven years go.

Jean gave the sunset and George's face equal time. She could see the forbidding beauty through the transparent dome, she could see the warm beauty in George's face. He had the uncanny knack of remembering only that which was beautiful. His dreams must have been filled with wonder.

"Yes, dear, I remember. The children were... " Jean couldn't continue. She found it difficult to even think about children, let alone talk about them. Where were they now? What sunsets were casting their alien rays on their youthful faces?

"Yes, dear. Now, at least they have the beauty of our early childhood. They can breath pure air, eat an apple from a tree without having to sterilize it. They can swim in a lake, like I still could eighty years ago. I sort of envy them. They are alive."

This was the first and almost the last time that George spoke about the children. They seemed more alive in his memories than he was within his own world. For the first time in months, perhaps years, his eyes shone with strange, wistful determination. As if he was totally committed to do something, no matter what. He said one more thing before the dinner was over. He said: "You know, dear, I visit them quite often. They are doing just fine."

Later, Jean tried to get George to tell her what he meant at the dinner table. It didn't work. The ephemeral spark which then, upstairs, glimmered in George's eyes was gone. He could hardly hear what she had been saying. He said he was tired, said he needed a little nap.

George woke up about an hour later. He was more cheerful then usually—seemed filled with extra energy. He got up and made herbal tea for Jean. She loved it. It was fresh from their upstairs garden. He then dialed the buttons on the synthesizer for some biscuits. How did he know about it? She never told him about the synthesizer. How did he know? He carried it all upstairs, himself.

This was the first cold night. Cold temperature was the only power which could dissipate the blanket of yellowish fog or the near perpetual cloud cover.

George sat on the same side of the table as Jean. He waited until the last, lingering shades of red disappeared from the western sky. He then blew out the candle flickering on their table and put his arm around Jean's shoulders. They used to sit like this, years ago, and watch the stars together. She remembered, vaguely.

Then, George raised his left hand and, with a slightly shaking finger, pointed northwest, towards the Lyra system.

"We call it Vega, he said. It is a big star. The fourth planet, they call Esperanza. The planet of Hope. Rather nice. I like it," he said, a wistful look returning to his eyes.

"They...?" Jean felt strangely secure with George's right arm holding her protectively.

"Why yes, dear. The children. Johnny and Brenda. The twins have also joined them. They are all together again."

Jean didn't say anything. She wanted so hard to believe in what George was saying. She wanted so hard to believe in anything. Anything concrete, less transient.

"You will join us there, want you?" George bent down and gently kissed Jean's gray, wispy hair.

The next day George slept a very long time. At noon Jean went to insist that he had to get up. He didn't. He'd joined the twins, and Johnny and Brenda.

Three days later, the Brothers assigned a wonderful, kind widow named Martha, to share the homestead with Jean. After Martha's husband, Brad, died, Martha felt a need for company. She failed to understand why Brad and she could not die together. It did not make any sense. At least not at the time.

The women had a great deal to share. They reminisced about many, many things only women talk about. Mostly when they are alone. They shared disjointed images of treasured fragments of their lives, meaningless to other people who never shared similar experiences. Sometimes the memories invoked a smile of recognition, sometimes a touch of nostalgia, shedding a furtive tear. On the third day, sitting upstairs on the garden terrace, Martha, a blissful, contented smile on her weathered face, said that her children, and her husband, were all waiting for them on Esperanza. So she said. She also said that it wouldn't be long now before they would be all together again.

"Why do you say such things? You don't really believe them, surely."

Jean had been more than pleased to share her memories with Martha but all this talk of dying was too much like some mumbo-jumbo she did not ascribe to. All her life she had been pragmatic. She had to be. She had a family to look after.

There was a momentary silence. Martha glanced at Jean, concern displacing serenity in her so worn, yet strangely lively features. She tried to find a way into the other woman's anguish. Could it be lack of faith? Lack of hope? Or just refusal to face facts as they presented themselves. Jean seemed attached to some old, religious concepts that, perhaps, were outdated. Only They could know for sure, and They, the Brothers, weren't talking. At least, not lately.

"Do you remember the first broadcast They made about a year after Their arrival?" The pronoun 'They' had been reserved, mostly, for the Brothers from wherever. After four years, still no one knew who or what They were, or from where They had come.

"How could anyone forget..." Jean smiled sadly. All her smiles had been sad these days.

"Well, you recall that everyone, no matter what language they spoke, they heard, and understood, what the Brothers were saying."

Jean nodded.

"The only way I can explain that phenomenon is that they were addressing not our physical senses but some other aspect of our awareness." Martha was searching for words.

"Then why use the communication media?" Jean was not impressed.

"Can you think of a better way to attract our attention?"

Jean had no idea what Martha was driving at. But, she listened. There was nothing else to do. No one to look after. Martha didn't really need any help. She had a heavy limp in her left leg, but it didn't stop her from being pretty independent.

"That was one thing. The second was when They refused Brad and me the transport to..."

"They what?" For the first time Jean sat up. "I didn't know They refused transport to anybody. Surely..."

"They did. I assure you, Jean. To be more precise, They said that I could go, but Brad had not been well enough. He had been quite ill for some time. Well, I couldn't leave him alone." There was no regret in Martha's smile. "But, don't you see, there were certain restrictions on those who had been given the new planets' option."

"I had no idea. I had no idea at all... You mean, you wanted to go and..."

"We both wanted to go. They explained, some people, mostly of a certain age, are so attached to their physical bodies, that they could not use the transporter. Apparently, an illness also tends to attach you to your physical body. Perhaps it attracts your attention? I don't know. Anyway, They said there had been nothing They could do about it. Not until such people vacate their bodies freely. By an act of their own will."

"How can anyone vacate her body?" Jean drifted back into a stoic acceptance of her fate—a brief spark of interest dissolving in the darkness of her melancholy.

"Do you remember how your children had no fear, no qualms about going into the completely unknown?" Martha tried again.

The spark returned. "Not even a whisper of fear... No concern about tomorrow..." How well she remembered.

"Their attitude translated into a state of detachment. Detachment means freedom."

There was a fresh glimmer in Jean's eyes. All her life she had been attached to her duties. She had born her fetters without complaint. In a way, she had tied the chains herself. Could it be that now, she would be free, at last?

"Just how do they transport people...?" Jean asked after a considerable pause. There was a smidgen of hope hovering at the edges of her mouth.

"No one seems to know. But it appears to be

some form of energy projection. Brad said that They were projecting life force. The stronger the life force, the greater the distance. There seems to be some kind of relationship. Then, at the destination, the life force can again express itself anyway it wants to. Or, anyway it knows how. Or it could be that They convert all of you into energy and the life force is only a, sort of, matrix, for converting you back into matter. I don't know! How could I? I am here, with you, aren't I?" And having said what she just did, Martha understood why she did not die, could not have 'died', with her husband.

This time the silence lasted much longer. Jean's eyes were losing their melancholy expression. A still hesitant, but a definitely growing gleam of life was wining over her past attachments. Mostly an attachment to old concepts, old ideas. Jean looked, as though she was waking up from a lifelong dream.

"Have you been inside the large sphere?" Jean asked suddenly.

"Yes. It is quite empty. Inside it, you are aware of neither space nor time. You seem to be alone—only with yourself." Martha said slowly.

"You talk to yourself?"

"I cannot really describe it. It is as though you were within an empty universe, which is waiting to be populated by you, to be filled with life. Your life.

Your thoughts. There is no sound. You just, sort of, sense the answers. In a way, to questions you haven't really asked."

"How does one get into the sphere?" Jean asked.

"I can't tell you that either. You just do. When you're ready."

In spite of herself, in spite of her lingering attachments, Jean thought she knew the answer.

"Thank you, Martha." Then she reached over and embraced her newly found friend. "How can I ever repay you?"

"I didn't give you anything you didn't already possess." Martha was basking within a strange feeling of freedom. Finally. A certain, inexplicable lightness of being...

"Esperanza. I like it. I like it a lot." Jean said remembering George's words.

"Perhaps, we shall be neighbors?" Martha mused.

"Perhaps. Soon."

They were both right.

***

Acknowledgments

I would be remiss were I not to thank my many friends who read the galley proofs and helped to make this book a success. Most especially my thanks go to those who having read it offered me their reviews. Also their diligent editing raised this anthology to an acceptable literary standard. Finally, my gratitude to my wife, Bozena Happach, who put up with being a grass widow for weeks on end and then allowed me to benefit from her insights.

Sincerely,
Stan I.S. Law

A Word about the Author

Stan I.S. Law (aka **Stanislaw Kapuscinski**), architect, sculptor, and prolific writer, was educated in Poland and England. Since 1965 he has resided in Canada. His special interests cover a broad spectrum of arts, sciences and philosophy. His fiction and non-fiction attest to his particular passion for the scope and the development of human potential. He authored more than forty books, twenty of them novels. His short stories, 'literary', though tending towards Visionary-Science-Fiction, have been published extensively.

Under his real name he published seven non-fiction books sharing his vision of reality. He also composed two collections of poems in his original native tongue in which he satirizes his view of the world while paying homage to Bozena Happach's sculptures.

***

The first Book of this anthology is Sci-Fi Series 1

INHOUSEPRESS

Montreal, Canada